Clarion Books
a Houghton Mifflin Company imprint
215 Park Avenue South, New York, NY 10003
Text copyright © 1992 by Florence Parry Heide
and Judith Heide Gilliland
Illustrations copyright © 1992 by Ted Lewin

Library of Congress Cataloging-in-Publication Data

Heide, Florence Parry.
Sami and the time of the troubles / Florence Parry Heide &
Judith Heide Gilliland ; illustrated by Ted Lewin.
p.   cm.
Summary: A ten-year-old Lebanese boy goes to school, helps his
mother with chores, plays with his friends, and lives with his
family in a basement shelter when bombings occur and fighting begins
on his street.
ISBN 0-395-55964-2
[1. Family life—Fiction.   2. Lebanon—History—Civil War, 1975-   —
Fiction.]   I. Gilliland, Judith Heide.   II. Lewin, Ted, ill.
III. Title.
PZ7.H36Sam   1992   91-14343
[E]—dc20   CIP   AC

HOR 10 9 8 7 6 5 4 3 2 1

Watercolors were used to create the full-color artwork in this book.
The type is 14 pt. Galliard.

Florence Parry Heide & Judith Heide Gilliland

———— Illustrated by Ted Lewin ————

SAMI AND THE TIME OF THE TROUBLES

CLARION BOOKS · NEW YORK

My name is Sami, and I live in the time of the troubles. It is a time of guns and bombs. It is a time that has lasted all my life, and I am ten years old.

Sometimes, like now, we all live in the basement of my uncle's house.

Other times, when there is no fighting, when there are no guns, we can be upstairs. We can go outside: my mother can take my little sister Leila to market, my grandfather and uncle can go to work, and I can go to school.

The last time we had quiet days, my grandfather took my sister and me to the beach for a picnic. My mother came too. The sun was bright and hot, and we built castles in the sand.

"This is the way it used to be, Sami," my grandfather told me that day. "This is the way it was before the time of the troubles."

My mother looked at him then and shook her head. "It will never be the same," she said. I knew she was thinking of my father, and that we will never see his face again, or hear his voice.

My grandfather took my mother's hand. "It was an accident," he said.

"Accident!" my mother cried, though she spoke so softly that I could scarcely hear. "When they place bombs where people go to market? It is no accident when we die like that!"

They were quiet a moment.

"Will you help Leila and me with this sand castle?" I asked my grandfather. I did not want Leila to hear them talking.

My grandfather touched my mother's shoulder and then knelt down beside my sister and me.

"We can build the finest castle in the land," he said.

"But it won't last," I told him.

"It will last in your head, Sami. Just like today. And look, this is a beautiful day."

My grandfather was right, it was a beautiful day.

Today is one of the bad days. It has been bad for a long time. We cannot go outside at all because of the gunfire in the streets. My sister Leila does not leave my side.

I think about the fort that I built with my friend Amir the last time we were outside. I wonder if it is still there.

Now, in the basement, my uncle tells a funny story and everyone laughs.

I lie on the mattress where Leila and I sleep and look at the carpets on the walls. My uncle brought the carpets here from our house, because my mother says there must be nice things around us to remind us of the good days, to remind us of how it used to be. This is the reason we have, here in the basement, the big brass vase that was a wedding present to her and my father.

"There is so little space, why do we need this?" my uncle asked as he carried it.

My mother did not answer him, and the vase stayed.

My grandfather starts to talk. He talks of the day of the children. He speaks to everyone, but he looks at me.

I have heard the stories of that day many times, but I like hearing them again now.

Still my grandfather looks at me. It seems that he wants me to answer a question, a question he has not asked.

What is it that he wants me to say?

Suddenly there is a loud, hard crash that shakes the walls and makes the carpets tremble. I am afraid.

My grandfather smiles at me and I am not quite so afraid.

"Too close, too close!" cries my mother. She puts her head in her hands.

Everyone is silent, waiting, and my mother comes over to our mattress to hold Leila. My grandfather says, "Remember the sunsets we have seen? Remember how the sun seems to touch the earth? So close, so close. Yet the sun is millions of miles away."

In a moment he and my mother join my uncle around the radio on the other side of the room. They hope to learn something, they hope to hear good news.

I listen to my sister's soft song, a song my father used to sing, and I think of my father's peach trees. I remember his telling me of his trees many times, the trees of his orchards.

I try to think of them now. I try to pretend I am my father walking up the winding road, climbing up and up through the foothills, coming upon his orchards, the trees heavy with peaches, peaches like little rounds of sun. I wonder if those trees are still there. I wonder if I will ever see them.

The guns are loud, but the crashes are not as close as before.

I sleep, even though the noises of the night are inside my head, pushing everything else away.

We have many nights, many days, like these in this time of the troubles.

It is morning. My mother, uncle, and grandfather are gathered around the radio listening. Perhaps they have been listening all night.

My grandfather turns away from the radio and motions to Leila and me. "We can go outside now," he says. "It is safe."

My mother closes her eyes. I know she is remembering my father and worrying now, too, about Leila and me. She makes us wait until we hear the usual noises of the street before she lets us leave the basement.

I step outside. The air is dusty, but the sky is blue. I had forgotten the blueness of it! And there is more green. Each time we go out, there is more green. My uncle says nature is trying to cover up the sad ruins of the buildings, trying to cover up what the fighting has done.

I must help clean up, and I have brought the broom from the basement.

But first I go to the place where Amir and I built our fort. It is gone now, and I am sad. It took us a long time to build it. It was a good fort, it was strong and good, and I am sorry it is gone.

Maybe Amir and I can build another one, after we have helped to clear the sidewalks.

Already the streets are filled with people working, talking, buying, selling. Chairs have been brought outside again and the old men are sitting with pipes and newspapers, drinking coffee.

It is always a surprise, and my mother is always pleased, that there are so many things to buy after a bad time.

The day is noisy with the safe sounds of hammers and saws, of carpets being beaten and cleaned, of car horns honking, people calling.

As I sweep, a wedding party comes down the street. I wonder if my mother and father's wedding was like this.

My uncle takes the broom from me. "Go and play," he says. "The day is short."

I look for my friend Amir in the next street. He is there, safe. He is helping his father carry a mattress to their basement. "I think we will not be outside for long this time," says Amir's father. "We must use the time we have."

As soon as Amir is free to play, we build a new fort next to one of the fallen buildings.

It is not as good as our old fort, but it is good enough for today. I find a piece of wood that looks like a gun and help Amir find one, too.

"My brother has a real gun," he says.

We run, we hide, we pretend to shoot, we pretend to die. I see my mother at a stall buying flowers, and she frowns at me. She does not like for me to play this game.

After a while, we stop to rest. Amir says, "When we are older, we will have real guns."

I shake my head. "The fighting will be over then. It cannot last forever."

"But who will stop it?" asks Amir.

Two men walk by carrying little children on their shoulders. Seeing them reminds me of the stories I have heard about the day of the children. It was a long time ago, so long ago I cannot remember. I was younger than my little sister Leila is now. Amir and I have talked of that day often, even though we cannot remember it ourselves.

نعم للسلام

العنف

It was a day like today, a day when everyone could be outside, a day when the guns had stopped.

Without warning, children appeared in the streets. Hundreds and hundreds of children started to march. They carried banners and flags, they carried signs, and the words written on them said: *Stop. Stop the fighting.*

ARRÊTEZ LE COMBAT

The smallest children, like Amir, like me, were carried on the shoulders of their fathers. People lined the streets to see, people filled the balconies. They cheered, they laughed, they cried.

It was a day to remember, the day the children marched.

My sister comes to me. She tells me my uncle needs me, needs my help. As I follow her, I look back at Amir, standing next to our fort. He looks so tall! He stands so still!

STOP THE FIGHTING

STO
STO

The quiet time does not last long. Now we are back in my uncle's basement. The night rocks with noise, the air shudders.

My mother has bought a peach in the market today for Leila and me to share. My grandfather turns the peach over and over in his hands and says, "Where would anyone find such a peach at a time like this?"

I think again of the orchards of peach trees my father loved so much. Now I know they must still be there. Someday I will go to see them. Someday, when the fighting has stopped.

Suddenly I know what my grandfather has been silently asking me. And I know the answer.

I turn to him. "We can have another day," I say. "We can have another time when the children march in the streets."

My grandfather puts his hands on my shoulders, and I see that he is proud of me.

"Yes," he says. "It is time. Maybe now the ones who fight will hear, maybe this time they will listen. Yes," he says again.

In a moment he joins the others gathered around the radio, and once again I wait for the noises of the night.